LEOPARD
IN THE
CITY

LEOPARD
IN THE CITY

AN URBAN FABLE

BY
THOMAS K. SHOR

ISBN: 9780999291887

CITY LION
PRESS

Preface

In essence this book is autobiographic. It was born of the feeling I sometimes have when living in a modern Western metropolis and I turn a busy corner and suddenly feel trapped in a world entirely of human creation, a world in which nature, the wild and the free are banished. Like a leopard who suddenly finds himself so far from his native jungle, I find myself scanning left and right up the road: where are the mountains and how do I get back to them?

Finding myself with no way out of the city, at least for extended periods of time, I turned my longing and alienation into this story of a *real* leopard, an actual leopard of the jungle, who finds himself in the center of a modern city—very much in need of a miracle.

While the city in which these events unfold is imaginary and could be any modern metropolis, the book is richly illustrated with photographs from the city of Vienna.

And though the city is found on no map, can we say for certain that the leopard is also but a figment of someone's imagination?

Who knows—he could be you or me.

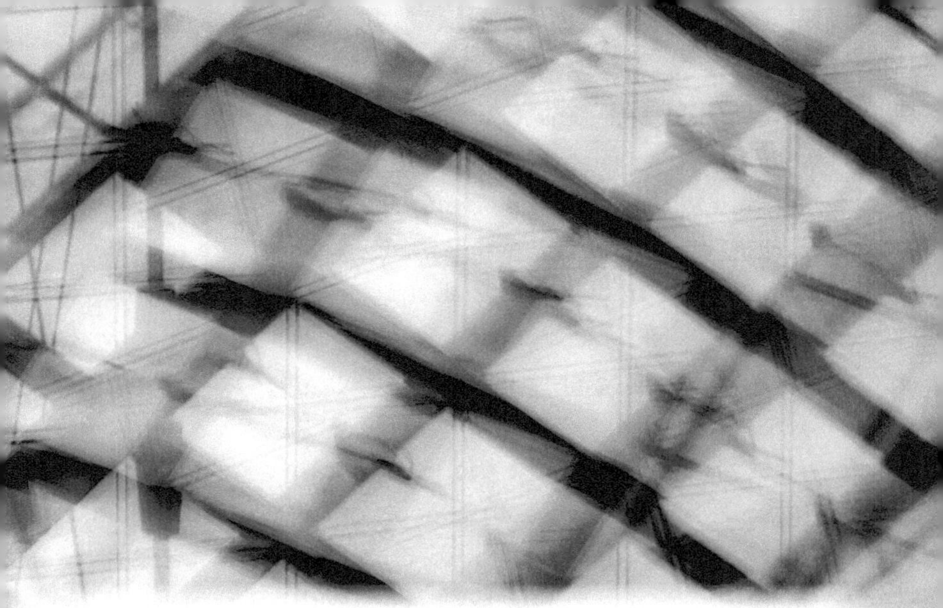

Don't ask how or why the leopard left its native mountains and found itself in the city. The important thing is that it happened: A leopard, senses attuned to the deep jungle, to steep wooded valleys and high mountain peaks, to streams and pools of still water, now found itself having to navigate the rigid grid of streets.

Being a leopard, his first instinct was to find a thicket into which he could jump. In the jungle it had always been easy to disappear, often in a single bound. There was always a bush or a patch of tall grass, or sometimes a deep ravine. The city offered no such place to hide. It was all straight lines and ninety-degree angles. Even the scraps of paper skidding down the street, which the leopard sniffed at as if they were blowing leaves, even they were rectangular.

In his previous life he had never known a right angle. And the only flat surfaces were the pools of still water the moment before he stuck his snout in to drink. He also knew the vast smooth velvet dome of the sky studded with points of light. Now when the leopard turned his gaze upward to orient himself by the heavens, still believing escape might be possible, the vault of the sky itself was washed out by the city's eerie glow and sliced by tall buildings into rectangular patches of what had once been the unbroken dome.

In the jungle there were no straight lines. Each branch was its own and no two were alike. There wasn't a single tree whose trunk rose without a curve all its own; streams meandered, paths followed contours.

Here, where the grid of streets ran straight and met at identical right angles, there was no way for him to disappear into the landscape as he was used to in the jungle, where no two places were alike, and with half a step, or a single bound, he could meld into the background, disappear, and be gone.

In the jungle the leopard could hide anywhere—even in plain sight. The proverbial leopard concealing itself behind a single blade of grass has its basis in fact. It works, but only if each blade of grass is different.

In the beginning, the leopard's nocturnal ways served him well. He ventured out only under the cover of deep night, when the human beings abandoned the streets and locked themselves into their multistoried residences whose ground floor windows were barred, apparently to prevent escape.

His first impulse proved true: to go to the river. But it was like no river he had ever seen. He had never imagined a city, let alone a river that had a great city grow up around it; therefore he had no way of knowing that a river could be straightened and tamed, channeled and confined between banks of laid stone, that there could be concrete canals backed by high brick walls and gleaming buildings built right out of its banks. In the jungle rivers had run wild in flood, hurling their way through the landscape down to the valley below. The sight of the river, mightier yet more sluggish than any he'd seen, was so strange and disquieting that he had to suppress a growl. He took his cue from the river with its straightened course and he restrained himself, not to give himself away.

It did not take long for him to find a large drainage culvert down by the river under a bridge and well above the flowing water's edge. It was not entirely dissimilar to the caves he had sought out in his previous life. Though in the very heart of the city, his new lair was a lonely place where no one ever went, tucked away under the bridge and difficult of human access. No human could ever have guessed what leopard's den now lay hidden in the city's ancient heart.

Knowing if he was seen it would probably be the end of him, he only left his den in the very dead of night when hardly a human soul prowled the streets. Hunger was his driving force, as well as the hope—still fresh in him—to find a way out and break free.

Those first nights he dared not venture beyond the river-bank, which abounded in rats. Rats became his sole source of nourishment. But for such a powerful and proud hunter as the leopard, hunting river rats that tasted of the dirty, lazy river was almost intolerable. Though he could take a rat down with a lazy swipe of a paw, though he could fill his belly, they would never nourish, not like the large game he was used to. No amount of rats could ever satiate the hunger that now plagued him. It was more than the hunt and the taste of large game: he yearned for the freedom that was his birthright.

He ached to hear the gurgling of water in the river bed, the roar of a waterfall; he longed to hear the rustling of the leaves. In the jungle there was not a single creature he feared. He lived in accord with the moment's needs—hunting when hungry, stretching out on a warm sunny stone on a frosty morning, sleeping in a shady grove when the afternoons grew warm, climbing a tree and laying on a branch and feeling the wind in his fur.

It did not take long for the rats on his side of the riverbank to grow scarce; whether he depleted them, or if after so many had disappeared down his prodigious gullet the others caught on and moved away, we'll never know.

Since rats, no matter how many he ate, could never fill the hole, it was perhaps not so bad that they grew scarce. It forced him to leave the safety of his culvert by the river and venture deeper into the city.

Hunting only in the dead of night under the cover of darkness, the streets were largely his. He was assured of being seen only by drunks and tired shift workers, those walking home, usually alone, through the deserted streets.

At four in the morning in large cities humans are cautious of each other, alert to sounds in the night and the drunks, thieves, and madmen who might be lurking in the shadows. On a few notable occasions those first nights someone did catch a glimpse of a suggestive movement in the shadowy depths of an alley. Once what was seen was a feline something passing in the dark space between lampposts. Another time it was a cat-like shadow. But every time somebody saw his shadowy visage and correctly took it for a leopard in the night, the shot of adrenalin-fear that would invariably follow could hardly reach the startled human's fingertips before what was seen was demoted to a phantom, and attributed to the weary hour and the tricks that eyes can sometimes play.

Human beings of the modern age, even when weaving home drunk in the middle of the night, are exceptionally rational beings. Their minds can easily override what their senses tell them. No matter how real the shadowy apparition appeared, how, they would ask themselves, could there have been a leopard—a *real* leopard of the jungle or the zoo—lurking in the predawn shadows of a sophisticated Western metropolis? And they knew full well the consequences of persisting, of believing in the apparition and raising the alarm: who would believe a tired somebody with such a story heading cautiously home to his bed, perhaps after a night at the pub, in the wee hours of the night? The very fact that it was well-neigh impossible for a leopard to be roaming the streets meant that he was protected. It was as if he wore a cloak of invisibility. Yet he knew, instinctively, that he couldn't rely on it.

Since human beings were out of the question, and the city was modern and well-managed and therefore had no feral dogs, food was a constant problem. In the jungle he had never gone hungry for long. Only sometimes in deep winter, when a storm overtook the mountains and the snow was deep and hard-going, only then did he know, and only for short periods, what it was to go hungry.

Each night the leopard's furtive search for other prey led him a little further into the grid of streets behind the river. Without leaving his refuge too far behind, he was still trying for a way out, hoping to find a place where the city ended and nature began, a landscape into which he could leap.

A few times when turning a corner or when passing the mouth of a narrow alley, he was startled by catching the unmistakable scent of his own kind on the breeze. Although it was unquestionably cat that he smelled, at the same time it smelled strange for a cat, almost human. He wondered, now that he was living in the human world, whether his scent was also changing.

Knowing there were others of his own kind as stealthily skillful as himself, sensed but not seen, meant he was not alone. Now he moved through the city knowing that around any corner he could encounter one of his own kind, one who, like himself, knew the silence of the forest, and who like him was padding unseen through the deep of night.

One night, shortly before returning to his culvert before the break of day, he smelt that odd, distinctive smell from down a side alley. He stopped and crouched, senses sharpened.

Then he heard the clang of a dumpster's metal lid. Curiosity, loneness, and longing got the better of him, for he knew the dangers. Hugging the side of the alley between the backs of old

13

brick buildings, he passed through the shadows towards the sound. And there, sitting on its haunches in front of a rusted green dumpster, illuminated by a feeble dangling light bulb, he found himself face to face with a tiny cat, a miniature, smaller than a leopard when born, yet apparently fully grown and mature. It actually looked quite wise with age, exuding confidence and self-possession, the size nor likes of which the leopard had ever known. She was a housecat, a gray-striped tabby.

Following the tabby's lead and emboldened by her fearlessness, the other cats of the neighborhood—who had scattered at the sight of this giant who had suddenly appeared, taking up an inordinate amount of space in their alley—began emerging cautiously from inside and under the various recycling dumpsters, from darkened basement stoops, back doorways and windowsill perches. There was awe in their eyes—curiosity mixed with lingering fear. The tabby remained sitting and was now calmly looking at the leopard. She seemed to be the leader of their little gang.

The tabby sensed immediately that the leopard, though obviously a wild cat, was not dangerous. She also saw the look of fear and displacement in his eyes, and his bewilderment at the sudden encounter. She understood his predicament and she took control.

"We'd better have a long talk before the sun rises," the tabby said. "When day breaks, where will you hide? If you are seen, even by a single human being, that will be your end. Humans do not tolerate many species in their city, mainly cats, dogs, and pigeons. The rest they kill. They will track you down and you will not get away. You *must* be off the street by the time it grows light."

The tabby's immediate grasp of the danger he was in gave the leopard his first indication of just how clever housecats were, how conversant in the ways of human beings. He was later to discover that housecats even know how to jump on a handle and open doors. In the jungle, the leopard could never have imagined what a door was—nor why, if it was shut, you couldn't just go around it.

"I found a place by the river," the leopard said, "it is round, like a cave. I go there before sunrise every day until darkness falls again."

"But even this is very dangerous," the tabby said. "By the look in your eyes I can tell you are new here. You don't know humans like we do. We've been living with humans for innumerable generations, ever since they first started gathering grain and building cities and attracting mice and rats. We know how to handle them. Contrary to what they'd tell you, *we've* tamed *them*. You should see how we live, how we have them answering our every meow, providing for our every need, feeding us, giving us shelter. But if even one human catches sight of you, even the tip of your tail or the glow of your eyes in the darkness, if they gauge their size and the distance between your pupils in the black of a back alley, you cannot imagine the furor that will be unleashed. They will go wild. And they won't rest until they have either caught or killed you. And there is no saying which would be worse: if caught they will put you in a cage from which you will never escape. You'd probably end up in the city zoo and they'll flock, having read about you in the papers—the mysterious wild leopard caught right in their city center. You'd have to endure the curious staring at you from behind iron bars till the day you die. But it is quite likely that you'd never have to face the zoo: most likely you'd be shot on sight.

The tabby was so deeply moved by the leopard's despairing look that she came to a rash decision. "This might be risky and even foolish," she said hesitantly, "and too big a chance—but extraordinary circumstances call for extraordinary measures. There is an empty apartment one floor up from where I live. Nobody ever goes there. I can get you in the back door. It would be safer for you to hide out the daylight hours there than in your place by the river. It belongs to the elderly uncle and auntie of my human family."

"*Your* human family?"

"It's the family of human beings I live with."

The leopard's eyes grew large with amazement.

"They provide me with all the food I need and always make sure I have a warm place to sleep. They bring me to the doctor if I fall ill, love me, and generally treat me almost like one of their own; they even let me sit on their lap as they stroke me. They gain pleasure by hearing me purr, so I purr for them to continue; and if I fall asleep, sometimes they remain seated so not to disturb me."

This last detail—about sitting on a human's lap—the leopard found difficult, at this early stage, to believe.

"The old couple from the apartment," the tabby continued, "can no longer travel. They live in another city with their children and grandchildren, so the apartment is empty and all but forgotten. My job is the mice, and to that end I am allowed to enter the apartment whenever I want through a back door that is left slightly ajar for the purpose."

Though it was her own private hunting ground and the mice supplemented her diet well—and though she felt an echo there of the ancient, almost ancestral thrill of the hunt and the kill, not to mention the satisfaction of keeping the apartment mouse-free for her family—she was willing to give all this up for the leopard. And this even though she knew the panic that would ensue if he were discovered—the scrum of police and the press—and that the apartment would certainly be sealed to her as well, forever. But she felt towards the leopard as she would towards a distant ancestor, a great elder of her kind.

"There is a widespread belief," the tabby explained, "almost a distant memory, among housecats—though some say it is an urban legend. It goes that we housecats are descendants of a species of giant wild cat so huge that even the largest dog would quake with the fear of being eaten by it.

"The story goes that this was in the dim beginnings, when our distant ancestors made their first forays into the human world and began the long process of inuring themselves to humans and, as we would have it, domesticating them; after all, human beings do provide housecats with food, shelter, love—and more recently veterinary care, kitty litter boxes for our convenience, as well as tinned and dry food designed especially for our palate.

"While gaining a privileged position by the hearth, our early ancestors naturally had to cede quite a lot, such as the freedom

that came with being at the top of the food chain, the feared hunter of all and prey to none. They had to sacrifice the thrill of hunting large game."

The tabby went on to explain that by gaining security over uncertainty, regular meals and a place by the fire, they had to be astonishingly adaptable, even agreeing to become diminutive in size by employing an act of will admittedly not in keeping with evolution as presently understood by humans. Yet they did it, they willed themselves smaller in order to move to their privileged position inside. Some say it took many generations; some say it was achieved in one. At any rate, they successfully transitioned from rodent control in the granaries at the emergence of agriculture and human civilization in Egypt and Mesopotamia, when there were grain surpluses to protect, to their privileged life of leisure with a secure place by the fire.

Bartering power and freedom for a secure existence, all they had to do in return was what they did best and was commensurate with their now-diminutive size, especially at the beginning: they made themselves useful by hunting small game, rodents such as mice and rats. Though this is no longer a necessary service for the vast majority of housecats today, it is a skill that is kept alive as a sport amongst modern city-dwelling cats.

"Pity the unfortunate cat living in a rodent-free city tower block," the tabby said with disdain, "whose swipes of a paw are reduced to the lackadaisical pursuit of flies, or worse—crumpled balls of paper!

"Now that we modern, city-dwelling housecats have evolved beyond the requirement of hunting for our living, all we are required to give back today for our food, shelter, and comfort is a minimal show of affection. In this we believe ourselves further advanced than the dog; we cats demonstrate a level of aloofness a dog could *never* get away with. And so it was that when it all began, our ancestors were as large and wild you are."

The tabby explained all this to the leopard, who now stood so displaced and so alone before them.

Then she told him how housecats cannot agree on how or where the first cats (or *fore-paws* as they fondly call them) appeared amongst humans.

"Naturally, Persian cats believe this first contact happened in the forested mountains of Persia south of the Caspian Sea; Siamese say it was when early humans made incursions into their jungle territory in southeast Asia, and cite the continued existence of leopards there as evidence. And in Egypt, where cats were worshipped and even mummified like pharaohs, we can guess where they believe this happened. You would be astonished to learn how many Egyptian cats still believe they are direct descendants of the sun."

The tabby was quite cosmopolitan in outlook. Her family was well read and intellectual, and she was often present on someone's lap while they debated ideas. Her opinion was that it was simply beyond housecats' ability to know their origins, that a species cannot fundamentally understand itself. It was her contention that a local, breed-based sense of primacy would lead only to endless cat fights similar to, though with far less devastating consequences than, the wars humans regularly engage in, especially when they dispute which tribe's god is supreme and who amongst them are his beloved children.

Not holding herself or any cat above any other, she still believed in the widespread notion that all housecats descended from wild, proud ancestors, now practically mythological not only in size, but also in character, the unmolested and uncontested kings and queens of the jungle. At that time, when they first made contact with human beings and realized the use these strange bipeds could be put to, they were a race of giants, some say even larger than the lions at Trafalgar Square, which were the largest any cat living today had ever seen. It is upon this proud ancestry that cats often dwell when deep in meditation and they seem so far away, even with eyes wide open. This also accounts for the cats' proverbial aloofness.

The tabby explained the difference between the wild and the tamed, and how human beings are quite particular, demanding of their housecats nothing short of complete domestication. She explained that while being as aloof as you pleased was tolerated, at the first sign that a cat was acting in accord with its wild, original nature, it would be accused of having rabies or distemper and be killed, or 'put down,' as they euphemistically say.

"And if it didn't get you outright killed," the tabby said, "you would certainly be out on your ear, cast into the life of an alley cat, having to scavenge meals and shift around for shelter, all the while despised even by your domesticated brethren.

"To us housecats, being *feral*, having gone wild from a domesticated state, is worse than being labeled *wild*. Wild is what our proud ancestors were. We housecats have tremendous respect, and even secret envy, for all animals in the wild; we admire their ability to live and prosper without dependence."

The tabby explained that the vast run of housecats turn their envy into hatred, and consider a cat that's gone feral as a traitor to the cause of domesticating humans, lower than low, an alley cat to be looked down upon for its matted fur, protruding ribs, and the festering wounds and scratches it continually acquires from scrapes with other ferals over food, sex, and shelter. While the tabby sympathized with the plight of alley cats—she even had friends amongst them—still she knew how difficult it could be to live in the human world without their protection, as she was sure the leopard was now coming to understand for himself.

Until this point the leopard had had no notion of *wild* because he had never had the concept *domesticated* to oppose it. He now realized that every animal he had encountered in the jungle—from the birds to the bears to the species he hunted and therefore had intimate knowledge of—was each simply following its own nature and not the nature of another species and therefore was *wild*, exactly that which would have to be eliminated, according to the tabby, to survive the human world. Domestication, adaptation, the willingness to be tamed: that's how the tabby's ancestors got her into the cushy situation she was now in, and that is what the tabby counseled him to practice, until he'd be fit to live in a human home.

"As a housecat," the tabby told him, "you can go as far as hunting mice and occasionally bringing entrails home as trophies. But you can go no further. You must understand: first and foremost humans domesticated themselves, they have subdued their *own* nature—they call it being 'civilized'—and they demand no less from any species that would live under their roof. Acting in accordance with one's true nature, whether one is a human or a four-legged friend, is never tolerated.

"To avoid conflict, at least within themselves, most housecats find it best to put to the back of their minds this memory of where they've come from and their innate wild nature. They do dwell upon it, but only in silence without betraying it to their humans. They do so while staring meditatively into space, perhaps when enjoying the fruit of their domestication curled up next to the fire or on a windowsill overlooking a birdfeeder, or perhaps on a warm lap after an easy meal of their favorite tinned cat food. At these times they are less likely to betray themselves.

"You, on the other hand: in your wild state, as huge as you are, it is only chance that you haven't been caught yet, and only a matter of time till you are. All it would take is for one human to see you, and this can happen any moment. One of these back doors could open with a bleary-eyed human taking out his trash, and you'd be finished. They would evacuate the entire city center. They'd use dogs to sniff you out, and they wouldn't stop until they either captured or killed you."

The leopard hunched his shoulders in a futile attempt to appear smaller.

The tabby continued: "The only way for you to survive the human environment is to go the way of the housecat and voluntarily forgo your wild nature and allow yourself to become both diminutive and domesticated. The city is so big that you'll never find a way out and back to your jungle. The grid goes on and on. So you must adapt. Allowing human beings to feel themselves superior is only a game, as any housecat knows.

"Who, after all, is serving whom? They provide us with food, water, shelter, health care, a blanket to sleep on, protection against fleas, even catnip to keep us happy, you name it. Better to be aloof, silently bearing the knowledge of your superiority, having adapted a species to cater to your every need. Human beings understand this on some level and feel discomfort at our aloofness, in which they sense—but cannot admit—our superiority. Yet on some level they understand. They sometimes wish we'd be more servile and needful—like dogs. Still, they put up with us; they even serve us. Human beings, when it comes to other species, often fall into arrogance. Only by appeasing them, by appearing dependant, do humans agree to see to cats' every need. It is a small price to pay."

The tabby felt justified being so forthright since it was only by fully realizing his inescapable predicament that she believed the leopard could muster the determination required to follow the path of her distant ancestors, who willed themselves smaller so they could better fit the new position they were creating for themselves in the order of things.

The tabby outlined her grand plan for the leopard. She explained that upon realizing the mortal danger he was in and that domestication was the only way, he could then gather the force of will necessary to actually make himself grow smaller day by day until finally he was no larger than a well-fed housecat. She was sure he could do it. In the meantime, he could lie low in the old couple's apartment. Once he became small enough, and once she taught him some manners, the tabby could take him home as a stray, at which point she was certain she could get her family to adopt him.

The tabby explained that since humans, the original domesticated animal, the creators of the concept itself, are less

adaptable than cats, it is up to the cat to adapt, as her ancestors did, by becoming smaller, by trading the stalking of large game for rodents, exchanging pride for comfort.

The tabby argued that least he think the housecat's position was lowly, it was really quite refined, even when compared to the dog. As evidence she brought up the problem of bodily waste and introduced to him the concept of kitty litter, a solution far more elegant than the dog's, who had to be taken outside each time, even down long flights of stairs, to the sidewalk or into the wilds of the city park with his human one step behind, plastic bag over his hand as he stoops down to pick up his still-warm shit or risk municipal fine. And even despite this, despite human beings having to supply kitty litter and clean it out, even though it is the human being that bags their dog's shit, and not the other way around, humans still believe they are superior, even to the dog. And this, even though they are the ones rushing out the door in the morning while their pets doze in the sun. Isn't it the human being that comes home tired having worked all day to keep the home they supply for their pets away from the bank and to provide food in all of their bellies?

"The *true* king—of the jungle or otherwise," she opined, "does not rely on hunting for his own food. How uncivilized and primitive that would be! He has it brought to him on a dish. It may be of gold or ceramic or plastic, but his food is served to him. Of course housecats, like so many human aristocrats, still hunt for sport, and even eat what they kill—but it is certainly not out of need. The pride of the cat in the jungle," she concluded, "was nothing next to the accomplishments of the housecat, who need not toil."

The tabby understood the immense significance of the en-counter for housecats everywhere. Since previously no house-cat, at least none she had ever met, had with their own eyes seen a cat significantly larger than themselves—let alone of such legendary proportions—the idea that they were descended from a cat larger and more powerful than any dog in existence took on epic, mythic dimensions and hovered prominently in the minds of housecats everywhere, even amongst the most punishingly domesticated, those well-groomed long-hairs that have the indignity of being harnessed and led by a leash like a dog down the fashionable streets of New York, Paris, Tokyo, and the world's other major cities.

And since none of them until now had ever seen a huge cat, it was an endless source of debate. There were always those who believed in their large-cat origin, and others who didn't. Some went so far as to doubt not only that they were descended from large cats, but doubted that large cats had any more substance than the dragons and monsters their humans once drew on the edges of their maps.

Disbelieving cats thought the believers were weak-minded and lazy-brained to believe—just because dogs were their perennial antagonists—in a cat with the size and power to make easy work and dinner out of even a pit bull or a German shepherd.

The tabby had always maintained that it had nothing to do with dogs. She reasoned that just because one has never seen a thing doesn't mean it doesn't exist. How else, under the sun, could anything new be discovered? She just knew—deep down in her bones, with no recourse to rational explanation—that they were descended from the intelligence of the jungle and that a majestic nature of tremendous stature was squeezed into their now-diminutive form, so diminished that their only defense against even the tiniest dog was a swipe with a sharpened claw before retreating up the closest tree, if they be luckily enough to find one.

The tabby, having always believed in this grand descent, felt compelled to save the leopard, this revered, if distant, ancestor come from afar, from another time and place. So she did everything in her power to persuade the leopard that it would be safer for him in the apartment upstairs than in his culvert. She explained how it would be much more comfortable as well.

The leopard, to this point, had had no notion of comfort since there was nothing to juxtapose it. He would have been wildly content to sleep on a bare stone boulder, if only there was one, or on the rough bark of a thick horizontal branch of some ancient tree with moss like a beard growing beneath it. He had known no more of the concept of comfort, which the tabby assured him was his to gain, than he had known of the concept *wild*—that which he'd have to give up to live amongst humans.

The tabby, who overheard everything her family said and what was said on the news, knew that the human world was full of troubles. She explained how increasing numbers of people were going feral and had nowhere to live but on the street like alley cats, like stray dogs, and more were coming from lands far away where humans were fighting. It was only a matter of time before one of these humans found the leopard's culvert by the river, which he described as large enough for a human to stand in, and decided to take up residence.

The eastern sky, what could be seen of it between the buildings, was flushing pink. Day would soon dawn, and the leopard would have to be off the street or risk scandal. So the tabby implored the leopard to waste no time and to come now, before the sun rose, and follow her quickly to her building so she could sneak him up the back stairs and in through the uncle and auntie's back door, where she assured him he would be safe.

The sudden immediacy of the tabby's beseeching request sent a shot of panic through the leopard's body. He'd seen doors locked up for the night, and he'd wondered why humans so readily allowed themselves to be captured like that. He'd seen the bars on the ground-floor windows to prevent them, he assumed, from breaking out. Every fiber of his being called out to resist voluntarily forfeiting his freedom. He would not allow himself to be tamed!

Scattering housecats in all directions, he fled up the alley in a single silent bound, leaving the cats stunned and deeply moved, knowing that even if they never set eyes on the leopard again, even if he vanished forever, they had witnessed something of profound importance for housecats everywhere, a vindication of their highest dreams, something they could take comfort in as they leapt on laps and accepted tender strokes from their humans. It was something they could meditate upon for years to come while purring contentedly: the certain knowledge that they had, indeed, descended from greatness.

The next nights the leopard stayed away from the alleyway of the Lilliputian cats. As he prowled around looking for prey other than rat or mouse, looking for a way out, he was aware every moment of his precarious situation and the dangers the tabby had spoken of with the feral humans who might well encroach upon his den. Yet to take the tabby up on her offer and be drawn into a human dwelling, abandoned though it was, made his blood run cold and his hair stand up on end. Though he didn't know what a jail was, it would have been like checking himself in.

In his previous life he had had no concept of freedom because he had never known its opposite. Now, as he thought of what the tabby said, as he considered her very reasonable suggestion that the way to salvation was captivity, to be free was to accept subjection, and that safety was not to be found in liberty but in confinement, now that these ideas were planted, the concept of freedom was forming within him, and for the first time he longed for it.

He watched human beings a little closer now. Hanging in the shadows, he saw how they let themselves into the confinement of whatever lay behind those doors and barred windows. He heard them lock themselves in. He hadn't the tools to understand. Not yet. Yet he sensed housecats, with their domestication, were doing the same.

In the jungle, the leopard's territory was large and mountainous, with rocky, cloud-enshrouded peaks, forests and ravines. There were also valleys of tall pines. Sometimes, especially in winter when storms piled snow on the mountains, he would follow his prey down into the valleys, where there was less snow or where it came down as rain, where he found other prey as well. These were the only times, in his previous life, that the leopard came close to human habitation, especially to a particular mountain village at the base of a slope where deep forest met the edges of the first fields under cultivation. During the lean times of winter he was sometimes tempted to cross the edge of a field and pad silently into the village under the cover of darkness and move through the shadows in search of the easy prey he could smell on the cold wind, a goat, a dog, or maybe a lamb tied to a tree. But he had never crossed over; he'd always sensed the danger inherent in humankind. His hunger had never been great enough to risk it. The jungle had provided all his needs.

It was a few nights later, when hunger was consuming him—the hunger that so far the city could nourish no better than with rats that tasted like the garbage they ate and the sewage in which the poor unfortunates were forced to live—that he broke out of his narrow territory, the grid of streets by the river, and he did what he would have done in the jungle: he set out in search of other habitats where other game might live, something that might prove more satisfying.

Thinking that the city might be like the jungle, and that more open space might yield larger prey, he found himself in the ancient heart of the city, which was the country's capital and had been even back in the glory time of the Empire. Here there were buildings of huge proportions, made of white marble with fluted columns and intricately carved niches and friezes. Here was the house of parliament and the various ministries, old buildings with large stone courtyards and ornate metal gates.

Though it was some hours before sunrise and the streets were deserted, the leopard could sense the power concentrated in the buildings of this ancient hub; he could feel the buzz of activity of all the humans who gathered there in the daylight hours, who populated the buildings and filled the streets with frenetic activity. But he could sense also that at night, at least in the time before the sun rose, the wide cobbled streets and broad stone courtyards were more empty of people than his place by the river, because here nobody lived. No one slept behind those locked arched doorways and entrance halls. The large windows with their heavy curtains opened to rooms with no inhabitants. So he felt safe to search out pray, to explore. Large buildings cast long shadows, and the leopard felt little danger passing through the city's ancient center with its plazas and wide cobbled roads.

And so it was, in the shadows of an ornate stone building that occupied an entire city block, that the leopard spied a huge eagle. It startled him to see such a powerful and wild hunter of the mountain air here, in the city, in the middle of the night—out, like he himself was, hunting.

The leopard, hugging the stone cobbles, moved forward with a liquid motion. He positioned himself for a surprise attack.

The eagle was looking down from an ornate plinth well within range of the leopard's spring. It must have been as hungry as the leopard. He must have spied a rodent. Its fierce claws were grasping a log. So intent on its quarry, so ready to swoop down on its prey, that like the leopard crouched unbeknownst before him, it didn't move a muscle. The leopard knew he had to strike fast.

Crouching low, his spine a coiled spring, the leopard crept forward. He knew well that moment of focused concentration before the pounce, the absolute stillness when not a breath is taken, eyes fixed on the target.

A leopard's element is stealth and his method, surprise. They reveal themselves, but only when it is too late for their victim.

The leopard sprang, fully expecting to catch the eagle by surprise. He knew well the eagle's sharp eyes and even sharper reflexes; he expected the eagle to shoot off for the heavens or defend itself with its razor-sharp claws and pointed beak. And though the leopard was ready to swipe the air to stop the ascending bird or to use his teeth to twist its neck, the bird did not move, even in that decisive moment between the time the leopard's powerful back paws left the ground and before his extended front claws dug into their quarry and his teeth hit their mark. And in that airborne moment, when intention became momentum, with his mouth open and his teeth exposed, flying through the air with his claws unsheathed, the leopard realized something was wrong. What kind of prey is this? Has the eagle lost its sharp instinct to survive? Will this be my fate too?

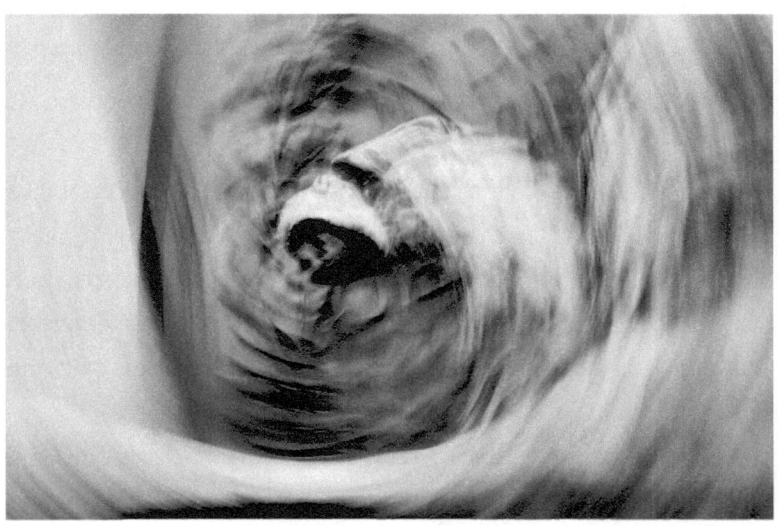

He hit the eagle with a force sufficient to take down a gazelle. But not one of the eagle's feathers yielded as the leopard crashed not into the flesh of an eagle, but into a block of stone carved to look like an eagle. It must have made a tremendous crashing sound. He lay stunned in a heap on the ground.

This marked the leopard's first major clash with human civilization, so full of things that aren't what they seem. In the jungle everything was simply what it was. Nothing seemed like what it wasn't. Never was there an eagle that wasn't an eagle. When you stalked an animal it never turned out to be a stone.

Fearing the attention his crash might have caused, he darted down the street of marble-façaded buildings, hugging the long shadows, dazed and disoriented, confused by his encounter with the stone eagle. The city never seemed more confining; his longing was never greater. If only he could break through the walls that surrounded him and go back to the jungle; if only shoots of bamboo would break through the cobbled street and transform it, if only tall grass would suddenly appear into which he could abscond.

The tabby's words echoed in the cavity of his rattled skull: Do as my ancestors did and forsake instinct; forfeit your wild nature and your place in the jungle. Come inside, and enjoy the comforts of human domestication.

The leopard swiped at the air as if to banish the notion. His entire being railed at the prospect, and before he could catch himself he let out a growl such as has never echoed off such marble walls before. It was the full expression of his defiance, and it echoed far into the night. He ran to escape it, least anyone chose to investigate.

The sky between the ravines of buildings towards the east started flushing pink. The sun would soon rise. He had to get back quickly to his culvert. But when he got there he first smelt and then saw a human being, a feral, a young homeless man from a land far away, inside his culvert rolled in a blanket to keep out the cold. His head was on a small brown plastic bag containing all his worldly possessions. It was exactly as the tabby had warned.

The leopard held in check the instinct to scare the man away, to retake his lair as he would have in the jungle, where he feared none and was feared by all. It would have been simple, a low snarl would have sufficed, and the man would have fled, never to return, maybe leaving behind some food in that plastic bag his head rested on.

Instead, the leopard withdrew and hid in some bushes in an untended back corner of a nearby park, which was overgrown and full of trash. He survived the day hidden in that thicket, and at night, long after the streets had emptied, he found his way back to the alley where he had met the tabby.

She was there, back where the dumpsters hid in the shadows, as she had been every night since they had met, hoping he'd come to his senses and return before getting caught or killed. By the look in his eye the tabby knew he was ready to begin his transition.

She snuck him through the back alleys she knew so well to her neighborhood and up the back staircase and showed him how to open the uncle and auntie's back door, which though looked locked wasn't, and could be moved, even by the tabby, upon its silent hinges.

The tabby showed him around, a living room, kitchen, and a bathroom, two bedrooms, and a little front hall. He could move freely through the apartment, but he must not allow himself to be seen from the windows. She told him to maintain his soft feline step and not to knock into anything, for the slightest sound would raise the alarm since the apartment was supposed to be empty. And she warned him that if he were detected the situation would quickly escalate beyond her control. She was putting him into the situation; if things went bad, she was only a housecat and wouldn't be able to get him out.

With daylight soon approaching, the tabby left for her family before her absence raised suspicion.

The leopard had never found himself inside four enclosed walls. He'd never experienced the oppression of all those flat surfaces from floor to ceiling meeting at those alien and precise right angles. They blocked his movement at every turn.

There rose within him an almost uncontrollable urge to leap, to crash through a wall as if it were a screen of leaves and to find himself back in the jungle, far from this concrete one of mankind's making, so full of such harsh and unforgiving lines and edges.

Most disconcerting was when he looked up to where the vast vault of the sky with its tapestry of stars and high tumbling clouds should have been; now there was only the low ceiling, off-white with cobwebs in the corners, dusty light fixtures dangling like the fruit of artificial vines.

He ached to achieve the miraculous, to break through these walls, to vault through the ceiling and scramble up a wooded hill, to disappear behind a tree or leap behind a bush—or yes, behind a single blade of grass, had there but been one.

He paced that night with precise figure eights through the rooms as if to wear an endless loop into the wooden floors, ceaselessly, round and round on his silent pads. It was well after sunrise when he fell into a corner of the living room and collapsed in a state of exhaustion.

This marked the leopard's first disquieting step towards living the ways of human beings.

The next morning after the tabby had her breakfast and a bowl of warm milk she crept up the back stairway, pushed open the door, and came into the apartment to check on the leopard. He was still fast asleep in the corner where he had dropped. The tabby sat on the arm of an old couch draped with a sheet and watched him sleep, troubled by her certain knowledge that he could be caught at any moment. She felt heavily the burden of responsibility she had taken on. His entry into the human world would have to be swift; there was no time to lose. When the leopard awoke, the tabby told him so.

"It's only a matter of time till you're found out; it could happen quicker than you think, at any moment, and that will be your end. So you must merge in as soon as possible. In order for you to adopt, adapt, and learn to enjoy the fruits of your domestication, you can no longer rely on my telling you about human beings' strange ways. There isn't time. You must start experiencing human beings firsthand. You must see for yourself. What I'm saying is that you have to start moving amongst them. And the sooner you come out of hiding the better."

The hairs went up on the leopard's spine. "Move amongst them—but I'd be seen! Are you crazy?"

The tabby led him to what was once the elderly couple's bedroom. She nudged open the closet door and rubbed against a long dark brown winter overcoat.

"If you put on this old overcoat you can go out on the street, even right now in broad daylight; just drape it over your shoulders; pull the collar up around your ears. They'll mistake you for a man. You know from the jungle how to pass unnoticed. I assure you, you can walk down the street and no one will notice you."

The leopard stared hard at the tabby. "But—how can this be?"

The tabby explained: "Humans are different from other animals. They have lived so long out of the jungle that their senses have atrophied. Their most basic senses, like smell, have been dulled by years of living in cities of their own creation. Things we can readily smell they can't pick up at all. They still have noses, but you can't imagine how dull they are. Even a mouse can sniff things out better than a human. Their hearing is much the same. If a human were to find himself back in the jungle, he'd barely survive a day.

"It is odd, but though their eyesight is still quite sharp, they tend to see what they expect to see, and not what they're actually looking at. They have too many ideas in their oversized heads. Once you understand this, you can use it to your advantage. Just remember: what a thing *looks like* is often more important to them than what a thing *is*. If they're not expecting to see it, quite often they simply won't. It's one of the strange things about them, one of the things you should know, one of the keys to understanding humans, necessary for navigating their world."

The leopard felt almost dizzy. "You're suggesting I put on the overcoat—and step out on the street?" He must have misunderstood.

"Since they fall so easily for the surface, the gloss, they are easily fooled; they even make an industry of fooling each other, and not only by selling each other things they don't need.

"One time a man came to my family's house and said he was a friend of the neighbors' and asked to use the phone, and then the bathroom. I knew immediately—I could practically *smell* it—that he was a thief and wanted to bring my family harm. What they saw was a well-to-do gentleman in fine clothes; they couldn't see that look in his eye that gave him away, that nervousness in his body. When I tried to warn them as best I could by arching my back, making the hairs stand on end, and letting out a series of plaintive meows, they thought I was being difficult, impolite, and inhospitable—and they put me outside. As it turned out, when no one was looking he stole money.

"I assure you: if you put the old man's overcoat over your fur no one will notice. They're in too much of a hurry—too focused on the commonplace of their everyday, too enmeshed in their daily routine, too concerned with what they themselves look like, their world of fashion. They really don't notice much else.

"To them, you'd probably be somebody shuffling by in an outsized overcoat. They'll probably take you for a vagrant and avert their eyes. That is what they call feral human beings: vagrants, the human equivalent to the alley cat.

"It won't matter, even that you have long whiskers—even if you walk on all fours; drape the coat over yourself as best you can. Cover your fur, but always remember your feline nature, your inborn ability to walk gently and meld into the background. Use their weakness, their propensity to confound, to your advantage. Understand their ways and you will find your place in their world."

Before coming to the city, the leopard had always been naked. But back then there had been no juxtaposed *clothed*, so the very notion of being naked did not exist. Now, for the first time, he understood the concept *naked*. It's what he'd feel if human eyes fell on him—even if, paradoxically, for the first time in his life he were clothed.

It took a few days and a lot of convincing, but in the end the tabby persuaded the leopard to don the old man's overcoat, go down the back stairway, step out onto the broad daylit streets, and mingle.

The leopard's first human encounter was a moment of crisis. What if the tabby was wrong? It was an old lady with a bag of groceries. The moment her eyes fell on him he was sure she'd scream and set off the alarm bells that would mark the end of his freedom and possibly his life. But she only eyed him suspiciously, clutched her pocketbook to her chest, and gave him wide berth.

Others passed with the averted gaze and discomfort humans reserve for someone of ill repute—like a dirty, unshaven vagrant. People just looked away and quickened their pace. One woman even took her young child's hand and crossed to the other side of the street.

With time he learned to blend in, and soon he was moving unobtrusively through the city, fluidly, attracting as little attention as possible, almost like a shadow hugging the periphery, nondescript, and promptly forgotten.

That said, he did have three close calls early on when his thin disguise catastrophically failed.

First was when a beefy biker with heavy leather boots, black leather pants, a leather jacket, gloves made of leather and even a hat to match came walking around a corner right in front of him. The biker was larger than most other humans, hairy, of tremendous girth, with multiple ornamental metal rings through his nose, ears, and his bottom lip. His neck was tattooed with the image of a howling wolf. The leopard had never seen a human dressed in the skin of another animal.

The biker was holding the end of a chain, at the other end of which, and coming around the corner behind him, was a German shepherd with a studded collar and blue bandana tied around its neck. The dog was huge, used to being a presence on the street every bit as menacing as that projected by its owner.

The dog, not being human, saw right through the overcoat to the beast within. He became a quivering mess, first trying to hide behind its owner, then pulling hard against his chain trying to break free and bolt around the next corner, its tail between its legs. For the first time in his life the mighty dog feared being eaten; for the first time the biker thought his menacing four-legged alter ego was a wimp.

His second close call was when he came upon a toddler taking some of his first steps in public with his proud mother. The child—as yet unhabituated to the way his parents saw the world, with one eye still in the magical world of childhood—immediately saw the large cat so absurdly dressed. Being too young to fear it, he started laughing delightedly and breaking from his mother's hold, running towards the leopard, arms outstretched, to play with the great big pussycat.

Horrified by her son's sudden attraction for what to her was a wild-looking, dirty old man, the mother grabbed the boy by the waist, and practically snarling, lifted the child in her arms and hurried away.

As she turned the corner and crossed onto the next block, she thought not so much of the strange man—cities *are*, after all, full of strange-looking men—but of her son, who had been so unnaturally taken with that wild man. She wondered in an off-hand way what was wrong with her boy—he did things that sometimes disquieted her—and whether, one day, he would need psychotherapy.

The third time the leopard's disguise was seen through was by a madman recently released from the asylum. Because his sight was still reasonably unconditioned by normalcy, he saw the leopard for exactly who and what he was, fled around the nearest corner, and started raving about the animal beneath the overcoat. He was shaking so vociferously that an ambulance had to be called. The men in white jumper overalls came, and he found himself being driven back to the asylum screaming the whole way that he was not crazy and that there really *was* an ungainly leopard walking down the sidewalk doing a bad impersonation of a human being.

Because it simply was not possible for an individual of another species to be walking down a midtown sidewalk wearing an over-coat, because it would obviously be absurd, normal people simply could not see him. Their reasoning, which trumped their perception, was that if it's wearing an overcoat it's obviously human, and to think otherwise would be crazy. He was transformed in their eyes into some variation of an ungainly, unshaven vagrant—like the biker, only more so—in an old overcoat three sizes too large, lumbering along with an uneven gait, a man with a wild and dangerous air, potentially deranged, the type that people tend to cross the street to avoid and certainly not look in the eye.

The leopard would have thought that dogs, being fellow animals in the human world and able to see clear through his disguise, would have been on his side. This is because he did not fathom the cat/dog divide. Dogs know their physical superiority over cats. That's why dogs chase cats and not the other way around. But they also know that it is only because dogs are bigger that they can send a cat fleeing up a tree. Size for size, dogs know the cat would win, that they are the more refined and better hunters. Cats' reflexes, of both claw and tooth, are greater, and dogs know it. That's why a dog catching sight of him would respond with hysterical barks at suddenly finding itself in mortal danger, as if the cat would have its revenge.

He could keep an eye out for dogs and reverse direction. If he saw a pram or young child he could cross the street. He could stay away from parks. But madmen proved more difficult to avoid. It was not easy to detect insanity merely by how somebody walked down the street. Even to the leopard's finely tuned senses the insane were indistinguishable from anybody else—that is, until they set eyes on him. They would see directly that in reality there was no disguise, but an overcoat slung over the humped shoulders of what was obviously a leopard trying to merge into the crowd of shoppers and people coming home from work.

Left with the impossible task of communicating what they'd seen to others without sounding like the stark raving lunatic they obviously were by the very fact that they'd seen the leopard in the first place, they'd go completely berserk.

So far, with people's attention drawn to the raving human being, the leopard never found it difficult to escape around the next corner. However, it always left him rattled.

The leopard was always looking for a way out, a place where the city ended and the green began, where he could find his way back to the jungle. One day, early on, he thought he'd found it when he got to a place where across the street it was all green with high trees, and an undergrowth of bushes, flowers, and grasses with a trail leading right into it. But what he'd found was a city park, and it was surrounded on all sides by the city.

While the city parks seemed to satisfy human beings' distant need for nature, it only reminded the leopard of the echo of what he had lost. He learned to avoid parks during the daylight hours, especially when the weather was good and they were full of people walking their dogs or taking their young children to play on the grass. Sometimes when the weather was bad, he'd don his overcoat and go into an empty park during the day so he could wander alone. But being strongly reminded of the jungle only added to his alienation.

It was only during the day that he donned the overcoat. At night he still had to hunt. Since even a rat would prove more nimble than he was under that ungainly thing, tailored as it was for human anatomy, he hunted naked, in his natural state. City parks proved a source of the occasional rabbit, squirrel, and duck.

With time, the leopard learned that he could venture into the large spiring buildings, the churches, and sit in a pew in the back, wrapped in his outsized overcoat for as long as he liked and not be molested. Hunched over, he looked like he was praying, or was maybe just an old man resting his tired bones. He was soothed by the smell of so much old cold stone, so reminiscent of the caves he had known in his previous life. It brought him a sense of peace, as did the paintings and old stone carvings behind the altars, in the niches, and under the domes, the winged and flightless human beings sculpted in stone, painted on walls, and illuminated by sunlight through colored glass. And high in the domes above the canopy of pillars, he saw long-bearded human figures flying through the air in flowing robes.

He was amazed by the depictions of humans with wings, the so-called angels. That's because occasionally, as he passed through the city, he had been baffled—as baffled as he'd been by anything in the city—by seeing a human being with wings. He had only seen them once or twice, and never being used. Stranger still was that nobody seemed to notice the wings, not even the one out of whose shoulders they sprang! Everyone acted as if the wings weren't there.

It was like his own disguise: the wings were invisible to human beings because human beings weren't *supposed* to have wings. And since they weren't supposed to be there, they were safe from detection. It was the same principle, after all, that allowed him to move through the city in broad daylight. Humans never would have believed that someone of another species, in his case a leopard, could at this very moment be sitting in the back pew of one of the city's central churches. They never used their wings because they weren't supposed to be there. Yet there they were, painted and sculpted, no doubt by human beings, in such numbers and variety in every one of these huge spiring buildings.

Sometimes when sitting in a pew the leopard would close his eyes and breath in the stone-cold air. He'd find himself back in the mountains' rocky heights overlooking the deep forested lowlands. Under the churches' high pillared domes he'd feel that living pulse that throbs through everything in the jungle, in the flight of the bird and the leap of the deer and in the bee finding its nectar in the flowers. In the jungle, the boulder was no less alive than the bird. The water bounding headlong into the valley did so with a vitality all its own. No less alive was the earth itself and the ground he walked on. In the jungle there was nothing that was not alive.

And even with eyes open, if he let his gaze range high above him to the paintings of the heavens and the mosaics in the round-domed ceilings, he experienced something close to that of looking into the canopy of the stars as he used to in his previous life, when he would go to promontories high above the pines—rocky outcroppings, sharp peaks of stony mountains—where his eye could range out over the roof of the forest and the unbroken arc of the sky. On moonless nights he would lie on a high stone shelf when the silent mountain vastness was illuminated by a deep star-studded sky. Lacking human understanding, he would have been unable to name the heavenly bodies or know how they were formed, the distances between them or their elliptical courses. But in these times he knew that the living pulse of the heavens was one with the pulse of life that throbbed through his body and gave spark to his own being.

With no concept of the demarcation of time, no minutes and seconds, no hours and ages and years and certainly no inclination to count them, the leopard had marked the passage of time by the sun's journey across the sky and the steady march of the stars.

If you were to pin a human label on what the leopard experienced in churches you might come closest by saying it was the sacred. But *sacred* is a human concept, and as such it is always juxtaposed with its opposite, in this case with the profane. What the leopard experienced was something greater, the sacred prior to any juxtaposition.

No matter how long the leopard spent in the oasis of a church interior, there always came the time when he had to get up from his pew, step outside, and find himself back in the city's grid. He'd feel like letting out a roar strong enough to put a crack in a dead brick wall through which he could slip, or a growl of sufficient strength to knock the hats off the heads of the good citizens of the city rushing by in their daily pursuits, especially those hats made of animal fur for which the old ladies of the city were so famous.

On the street he always sensed the danger, as if his head was constantly on the block. Dogs remained a persistent problem. They would bark, and no matter their size or doggy ferocity, cower behind their owner with such a shivering fright that attention naturally turned to the cause of the dog's strange behavior, in

this case a wild-looking stranger in an outsized overcoat. Even a tiny poodle in a knitted sweater on a short leash, prancing down the block sniffing at light poles beside its human and leaving its tiny mark, was now enough to cause a panic in the once-mighty leopard as he reversed direction and slipped around a corner.

In the jungle the poodle would have been an easy hors d'oeuvre, taken down with a lazy swipe of a paw after not much of a chase; here, in the daylit streets, in the sophisticated city where the leopard was not a leopard but had, at the tabby's advice, become the representation of a man, it could even be a well-coifed poodle on its way home from its professional groomer— the fresh smell of shampoo still wafting from it like a perfume, a new pink ribbon in its hair, and its tail sculpted into three tight little balls—that could give him away.

The leopard could have avoided this danger. He could have stayed in hiding all day in the old couple's apartment. He could have gone out only when the poodles of the city were sure to be behind locked doors, snug in their little doggy beds. He could have averted entirely the indignity and mortal danger of being denounced by a well-coiffed, beribboned poodle.

But he knew the tabby was right, at least in this one respect: to survive the human world—or, if it were only possible, to escape it—he would have to move amongst human beings and come to know them. It was the key to his survival. But it was also a race against time, to come to know them before they came to know about him and caught him or put a bullet through his heart.

He lived in a constant and probably well-justified fear that his flimsy disguise would suddenly and catastrophically fail. He imagined it would begin with one person seeing through their own clouded sight as they suddenly realized what was obviously before them, something belonging in the zoo, a circus, or jungle, but certainly not on the city street, and that this realization would be followed by a shriek and a street crowded with human beings suddenly fleeing in panic, leaving him alone and seen through, like that emperor who wore no clothes, fearing, now that he was seen, what they would do with him, the poison dart and metal bars that would follow, or the bullet and the eternal darkness.

He always knew that if ever the time came, just before he was either taken in or taken down, he'd shake off his encumbering coat and with it any pretense of being human and let out that roar he'd been suppressing so judiciously.

No matter how much the leopard explored the city, he could find no way to escape. No matter how far he ventured, the city stretched out farther still. The grid seemed to have conquered space itself and go on forever. There was no way he could outrun it. He could no longer imagine a place where the city played itself out and the wild began.

With no route of escape, the tabby's grand plan for him—that he learn the ways of human beings, subjugate his will to theirs, make himself diminutive, and let her take him home as a stray—was certainly practical. If you're in a cage and there are no gaps between the bars through which you can slip, what is a dream of freedom but a living nightmare? Is it not better to adjust and make the best of it?

The leopard knew the tabby meant well every time she tried to convince him that the life of a housecat was a good and comfortable life. But each time the leopard pictured shrinking himself to the role of a pussycat—sitting contentedly on some human's lap, meditating silently with a faraway look, recalling former glory—he rebelled. The rebellious force came thrusting up from so deep within him that it was beyond his control. He now knew what to call this force that wanted to let loose as a roar: it was the voice of the wild itself, untamed, uncontrolled, unrepentant. Luckily, he had learned to nip the roar in the bud; if left unchecked, if he allowed it to burst through his throat in a mighty blast of sound, it probably would have been his last.

One bright sunlit mid-afternoon when the leopard was feeling warm beneath his cumbersome overcoat, he was walking down a quiet side street when he stopped before a window, one of whose panes was broken. He noticed the flies buzzing against the glass of the other panes, furiously crashing against the clear glass, trying to escape the confinement of the invisible rectangular barriers. The futility of their endlessly repeated action and the ease with which they could find solution if only they'd retreat slightly from their furious, futile pursuit, if only they'd pause the incessant

banging of their heads and fly away from their impossible goal to look for other avenues of escape; only then would they feel the breeze coming through the broken windowpane; only then would the solution be as clear as sunlight, and only then could they simply fly out through the broken pane and back to freedom.

With time, the leopard learned how to read, not well, but enough to get by. This might sound fantastic, but to one whose senses are so finely tuned things are absorbed practically by osmosis. Many things are easy that might not otherwise be. He had to learn their language just to survive.

Once the leopard began to understand that a stone could be formed by human beings to represent an eagle, it wasn't such a further step to understand how human language functions, and thus the ease with which he learned the rudiments of reading. With language, one thing is still represented by another, in this case not a piece of stone but a sound, a unique combination of letter-sounds for a thought. T R E E for a tree, or the sound of a T bursting from between the lips followed by a short r-like growl, followed up by the long-vowelled ee.

Early on, when he was just mastering how the twenty-six movable letters combined and were arranged to create meaning, he saw a man walking down the sidewalk with a T-shirt stretched across his large chest with huge block letters spelling out the word *Animal*. The leopard still had trouble separating the word from the thing, so he easily mistook the *word* animal for *an* animal.

Maybe it was only a dark fantasy, but he was ready to pounce. He held himself in check. He did not begin stalking the man. He did not pounce. It would certainly have been the end of him. As the man drew closer, the leopard saw something written above the word *Animal* in smaller, italic script more difficult for him to read. It spelled out the word *Party*. Peering out sideways from under his overcoat, the leopard wondered what exactly was a party animal? Did it really walk on two legs like this man?

It is not surprising—since his eye was conceived and trained in the jungle—that the leopard missed much of what any human would see. He was, for instance, impervious to advertizing. He could not have understood a simple arrow painted on a wall.

His vision was naturally tuned to other things, things he could relate to, and since there was little undergrowth in the city, his eye was drawn mostly to what a human might not so readily notice—the many animals with which the city was populated. They were made of stone and metal and were adorning buildings and archways and public monuments; shop windows had stuffed animals in them; there was the cow in the dairy window, the teddy bear playing nurse at a pharmacy, the owl wearing thick glasses at an opticians, even stuffed animals looking out of children's upper-story bedroom windows.

What strange creatures, these human beings, to banish all the animals from their creation—except for a select domesticated few, mainly cats and dogs—and then repopulate it with so many stuffed ones, ones carved in stone, pressed in plastic or sewn cloth!

At this stage, how could he have known the meanings attributed to the animals depicted, the answer to the question *why* they would fashion an eagle out of stone and place it looking down on the street. He knew nothing of the eagle's place in human imagination, how the eagle is used on flags, medals, sculptures, coats of arms and on the official seals of countless emperors, despots, and other heads of state to symbolize the might of armies and the strengths of regimes and nations and the nobility of kings. There was nothing

like this in the jungle, where nothing was what it wasn't. An eagle circling in the sky could only be an eagle, perhaps signaling small prey nearby, or carrion, or perhaps even lead to a cache of eggs, if he could but find the nest and manage to climb to it.

Finding nourishment continued to be a challenge for the leopard. Though now living in the human world, he still lived by hunting; and though he was now surrounded by more animals than ever, of a variety and fanciful construction such as he'd never imagined, the irony was that he still had little to eat. The consummate hunter, he was used to sniffing out his prey with senses more subtle than those known by most humans. But here, apart from rats and mice, the animals he encountered had no scent at all; there was nothing for his sharp nose to detect. Nor was there a movement to catch his eyes, nor a cracked stick to perk his ear.

And though he now understood, almost like a human would, that these animals were completely devoid of anything that would nourish, on a cellular level his body still reacted like a leopard, as if these mere representations in stone, plastic, cloth—what have you—were real. His stomach juices would begin to flow and his heart to race. Each time he caught sight of a stuffed animal, one carved of stone or wood, or even one made of pressed plastic, he had an almost uncontrollable urge to crouch, glide low along the sidewalk, and pounce, the consequences of which, he knew, would have been catastrophic: not only was he bound to break a tooth and get badly banged up if it were a stone sculpture that was his quarry, but pouncing on a piece of civic architecture, even while wearing an overcoat, would be a sure and rapid road to his ultimate demise.

The animals did, however, prove useful to the leopard, for as the leopard widened his territory he navigated by means of them—turning left at a stuffed bear in a shop window, or right were a lion crouched above a door. He knew all the public statues, humans made of stone too, busts and those mounted on mighty horses, military heroes that frightened him by brandishing guns and swords.

Penetrating another species' thinking takes time. The leopard realized early on that what sets humans apart was not only the ordered grids and right angles with which they built their city; it was also the way they filled their world with images of things—things that appeared to be what they weren't, like a piece of stone impersonating a man's head. The leopard realized that by donning this most ordinary of men's overcoats he was taking his first step towards his own domestication. It seemed a prerequisite to find one's place in the human world: to be something that one wasn't.

Over time, would he forget the jungle? Would he forget what it was to be free, that wild nugget within him, raw as any

uncut stone? Would he have the strength to will himself smaller to facilitate his move indoors, to take his place by the fire like a pussycat? And if he did, would he then take the image for the real? One day would he look into a mirrored shop window and mistake *himself* for a vagrant?

One fateful day the leopard found himself back in the area where he had had his encounter with the stone eagle, where the white marble buildings stood stately around cobbled court-yards and wide streets at the city's ancient heart. That had been the same night he lost his culvert to the feral young man and started the tabby's course in domestication.

He found it, the very stone eagle he had crashed into. It was still perched in its niche with its talons still gripping a log. He kept having this unnatural expectation for the stone to flap its wings and take flight.

As he looked at the stone eagle, he both marveled that such a short time

ago he had actually taken it for real and wondered—as he wondered about all the other animals placed around the city—what it was doing there. How could he have known that they placed the eagle near the gate of that particular government building, which he had no way of knowing was the Ministry of War, as an expression of the might of those who worked within and the power they represented while warning those who would challenge them of the furry they would unleash? How should he have known that because owls have large eyes they have been a symbol of wisdom through countless ages and cultures and can now be used to sell everything from school notebooks to eyeglasses? He saw the two snakes wrapped around the winged staff in a pharmacy window. Did snakes really dance to their tune?

In the jungle, a sudden cool breeze could signal a coming rain; the sound of a broken twig could mean the presence of a deer,

which in turn could mean a meal. The leopard was attuned to the jungle. His senses were many and they were all open. And though the jungle was full of signs and portents, everything remained exactly what it was. The movement near the river was either a deer or it wasn't. And while he shared the jungle with bears and birds, never was there a piece of stone that represented a

bear or a bird or could be mistaken for one. And certainly no fox was ever a synonym for sly. No pig was stupid, and no lamb was innocent. Never was there a bear that was the symbol for a country or a city. The docile cow was never preverbal. The bee was not known as particularly busy, and the snake was never the very image of evil. Things were simply what they were.

It is quite natural that of all the animals in the shop windows, advertisements, on public buildings and painted on primary school walls, the animals that he studied most closely were his large-cat cousins, the lions. Ever since the tabby described the relation of housecats with humans, the deal they had struck, he was still hoping for another way, a way to avoid the comfortable fate of the housecat. If only he could truly fathom the relation of the human to the feline, maybe then he would have the key.

Lions were everywhere, from lion-head door knockers to those guarding important buildings. They were carved into the keystones at the apexes of archways, depicted everywhere in stone and on paper, stuffed and cast in metal. His pursuit brought him increasingly to the old heart of the city where the former empire was administered and the concentration of lions was greatest.

He understood how a block of stone could be carved to look like a lion even though it didn't really look like a lion and could not (at least in broad daylight) possibly be mistaken for one. So he knew it was possible for there to be a lion that was not a lion, the same way, at least so far, he was perceived as a grubby, wild, and probably homeless, hairy vagrant and not what he actually and obviously was, a leopard, a wild beast worthy of being shot on sight.

It was through the placement of the lions that the leopard first came to understand that there is meaning attached to these representations. Not only could a piece of stone represent a lion, but lion itself could represent a quality, in this case supreme power and majesty. For there they were, so nobly above arched doorways, ferociously guarding important buildings, always at the place of honor, at the keystone of power, where otherwise one might expect a king to be. It seemed to offer confirmation of the tabby's contention that it was the cat that domesticated the human and stood supreme. That these large cats were depicted so fierce and powerful, exuding the very majesty of kings, sometimes even wearing the royal crown, gave the leopard hope and swelled his pride— precisely that quality humans attribute to the 'king of the jungle.'

He went to the Palace of Justice, the supreme court of the land, where huge, ferocious lions of the size to swell any feline's heart flanked the front entrance. Lions were everywhere, on cornices and at the heads of ornate columns, guarding the most high,

be it of state or private property. To pass through important gateways and grand wooden doors was to pass beneath the head of a lion at the arched apex.

It confirmed the leopard's innate sense that the wild reigned supreme, and that the unbound, the undomesticated, would always be far above the tamed.

For the humans themselves were tamed and controlled. They were all tamed, every last one of them, yet what lion could be tamed? The tamed worshipped the wild and the free!

Soon he was seeking out more lions. He found them on coats of arms and flags and atop doorways that even he could tell were entranceways to the highest seats of human power in the city.

It swelled the leopard's heart to see his kind placed above the kings of men, so regally, so often crowned, with jaws open mid-roar. This pursuit, to penetrate the true relation of the feline to the human, became his overarching aim. He sensed in it the key to his salvation, as if by fathoming the link the tabby first spoke of, between the housecat and the human, and their relation to the large cats of the jungle, he would somehow unlock the door of his confinement.

He was standing before a wooden door of tremendous proportions, large enough to give entrance to a king's carriage. He was admiring a lion's head circled by a huge mane in the center of the door all in gleaming golden brass, projecting itself forward with its fierce mouth open, when he noticed something he somehow hadn't noticed before in his exuberance: the thick metal ring fastened through its mouth.

It was no doubt used to pull the door shut or to put a chain through to lock it, but the sight brought him back to the jungle, when it was winter and he would sometimes venture near the village of human beings at the jungle's edge. It was there on the margins of the human world, with his feet still in the jungle, overlooking from a distance the domain of man, that he first saw domesticated animals, oxen with rings through their noses being led through the fields by these strange bipeds, doing the heavy work of turning the soil. It had disquieted him to see an animal, both larger and more powerful than a human being, being thus subdued. Even though the ring through the mouth of the brass lion in the center of the door had a utilitarian purpose, and could even be used to knock on the door, still it was a ring through the mouth, and its message was clear, and the leopard suddenly got it. Though the lion is the king of the animals, at least by the human conception, it is still subjugated to humankind. The price of disobeying was demonstrated by the torturous iron ring fastened through its nose or mouth and the intense pain that must unleash.

He felt as if he'd just missed putting his foot in a trap.

He understood: the lions were there to demonstrate how even the highest force of nature did not reign supreme, but was conquered and harnessed and put into the service of human beings. After all, the lions were guarding the human seats of power and human treasures, not their own.

Upon the roof of the House of Parliament, spaced at even intervals, were a little army of half-lion/half-eagle griffins. The leopard had been fascinated by them but hadn't noticed before that each held one paw up in the ultimate gesture of submission, obedience, and training—like a dog when holding up its paw to 'shake hands.'

One huge lion was lying with its head erect, its mane proud, its mouth open as if with a roar, and its paw proudly atop an ancient coat of arms, claws extended. The message was now clear: the lion was saying that if you want to make off with this shield with my master's good name or bring harm to my human master you'll have to fight me first. Wasn't the lion thus employed as a mere security guard, fierce, but a security guard all the same? Wasn't the message precisely that our leaders and powers are so great that even the king of the jungle is subject to our rulers, to our human powers, to our institutions? Another lion had his paw protecting the national flag.

In the jungle the lion might be king, but in the city it could only be subdued, working for and dominated by humans, or having been shrunk into the body of a pussycat. It might be depicted with a powerful jaw set in a ferocious attitude with nostrils flaring; but there can be no pride in having that article of torture—the iron ring—threaded through its mouth or nose, not if its powerful paw is protecting human treasure, guarding not its own lair but the palace of the human king.

Then he saw a lion above a window with hollow empty eyes, depicted not as fierce orbs but as blank holes that gave it a ghostly look. Its forepaws were stretched unnaturally over two protruding pegs attached to fur that looked deflated. Its hind paws were looped through metal rings. The leopard shuddered to realize what he was looking at: it was the skin of a slain lion, brought back as a trophy to humans' superiority over the wild.

Little did the leopard know of the great hero of Greek mythology, Hercules, whose first labor was to slay the Nemean Lion, a lion of almost monstrous size and ferocity. Hercules drove the beast into its cave and after his arrows and sword bounced harmlessly off the lion's magical golden fur, he fought it man to beast and hand to paw and jaw to jaw. In the end Hercules strangled the lion with his bare hands. The strongest man and greatest hero of Ancient Greece had won the fight to the death with the most powerful of the beasts and stood triumphant. Using one of the lion's own claws, he cut the meat from the magical pelt that protected from arrows and swords, cured it, and returned, wearing it like a cloak over his shoulders; he wore the lion's head over his own like a hood. If Hercules had gone on all fours he probably could have passed himself off as a the

Nemean Lion no less aptly than the leopard impersonated a man by wearing the uncle's overcoat.

The moment the leopard realized he was looking at a slain lion's pelt, the ultimate symbol for man's complete domination over beast, he knew he had to break free before it was too late. He would never shrink himself to the size the tabby suggested. And though it was high noon and he was standing before the fortified gate of the Ministry of War, protected by lions and double-headed eagles, he shed the overcoat like a snake sloughing its old skin. It lay in a heap by his feet, a worn out outer garment fit for the rubbish pile. He was naked now before that august door amid all those shuffling in and out to their important duties. Not even an instant passed before a woman in a business suit holding an attaché case let out a blood-curdling shriek. Panic ensued. The leopard swiped his paw to scatter the shocked human beings who all started screaming, not quite knowing what to do. He gave a full-throated growl and slipped swiftly and silently around a corner.

Though he was still free, his unmasking had all been captured on tape. This had occurred, after all, outside the doors of the Ministry of War, which is carefully overwatched by multiple video cameras by a central command trained to follow a suspect across multiple screens.

They knew in which direction to send the police with their big rifles. Experts from the city zoo were called in and told where to bring their dart guns. They even got a net from a circus. It was a race against time. The press went into a frenzy. The old heart of the city with all the big government buildings adorned with sculpted lions and eagles and powerful men on horseback was locked down as tight as during a major terrorist attack.

Everything went as it was fortold by the tabby.

The leopard was pursued some blocks through the city with the cops at his heals carrying high-powered weapons. Then his way was suddenly blocked by a police van, one of those built to withstand riots, with wire mesh covering its windows.

This was it. People were leaning out from the safety of their upper-storey apartment windows amazed by what they were witnessing, in the middle of their city.

The leopard's eye was suddenly caught by a large billboard on the brick wall opposite. It was advertising a Chinese restaurant. He could read it: Bamboo Garden. The name was superimposed upon a grove of bamboo as peaceful and green as any he'd known in the jungle. If he ran fast enough he could just make it to the bamboo before the police fired their first shot.

His bounds were so long and graceful, so full of nature's majesty, that there was a collective gasp of wonder from those looking down from their dwellings, eyes wide open. And on the street the police were so awed that they paused before pressing the triggers.

The leopard hit the grove of bamboo with such a blinding force that what happened next the police could never explain. They could never explain how, after tracking the leopard down, they lost it.

No one ever saw the leopard again. The city center was kept under lockdown for some days, but what could they do? They searched the city's sewers and most distant alleys using lights and dogs. They even searched the culverts down by the river. But with no sign of its presence they had no choice but to call off the search and resume normal life.

Don't ask how the leopard found itself back in its native mountains, so far from the city. The important thing is that it happened: A leopard, senses attuned to the deep jungle, to mountain peaks and steep wooded valleys, to streams and pools of still water, found itself back where a bird was a bird, a tree was a tree, and a leopard could roam freely, light as the morning dew.

The End

Thomas K. Shor is also the author of:

A STEP AWAY FROM PARADISE:
THE TRUE STORY OF A TIBETAN LAMA'S JOURNEY
TO A LAND OF IMMORTALITY
(Penguin 2011 & City Lion Press 2017)

THE MASTER DIRECTOR:
A JOURNEY THROUGH POLITICS, DOUBT AND DEVOTION
WITH A HIMALAYAN MASTER
(HarperCollins 2014)

GANGES LAMENT
Black and White Photographic Portraits from the Sacred
Indian City of Varanasi
(City Lion Press 2018)

SCULPTURE GARDEN OF THE GODS
Animated Landscape Photography from
the Greek Island of Ikaria
(City Lion Press 2018)

WINDBLOWN CLOUDS
(Escape Media Publishers 2003 & Pilgrims Publishing 2006)

Writer and photographer Thomas K. Shor was born in Boston, USA, and studied comparative religion and literature in Vermont.

With an ear for unusual stories, the fortune to attract them, and an eye for detail, he has traveled the planet's mountainous realms—from the Mayan Highlands of southern Mexico in the midst of insurrection to the mountains of Greece, and more recently, to the Indian Himalayas—to collect, illustrate, and write stories with a uniquely personal character, often having the flavour of fable.

Shor has lectured widely on his writings and has had solo exhibits of his photographs in Europe and India. He can often be found in the most obscure locales, immersed in a compelling story touching upon fundamental human themes.

www.ThomasShor.com